BESTSELLING FICTION

- 1984 by George Orwell
  Fiction/Classics, ISBN: 9789380914947
- A Tear and a Smile by Kahlil Gibran
  Fiction/Classics, ISBN: 9788180320477
- Alice's Adventures in Wonderland by Lewis Carroll
  Children's/Classics, ISBN: 9789380914046
- Animal Farm by George Orwell
  Fiction/Classics, ISBN: 9789380914701
- Black Beauty by Anna Sewell
  Children's/Classics, ISBN: 9788180320095
- Demian by Hermann Hesse
  Fiction/Classics, ISBN: 9789387669567
- Gitanjali by Rabindranath Tagore
  Fiction/Poetry, ISBN: 9789380914886
- Selected Stories of Nietzsche by Friedrich Nietsche
  Fiction/Short Stories, ISBN: 9788180320491
- Siddhartha by Hermann Hesse
  Fiction/Classics, ISBN: 9789380914145
- Tales from India by Rudyard Kipling
  Fiction/Short Stories, ISBN: 9789380914411
- The Hound of the Baskervilles by Sir Arthur Conan Doyle
  Fiction/Classics, ISBN: 9789380914534
- The Light of Asia by Sir Edwin Arnold
  Religion/Buddhism, ISBN: 9789380914923

Search the book by its ISBN

The Book of Virtues

A Treasury of Moral Stories for Young Generation

N.K. SONDHI

GENERAL PRESS

Published by
GENERAL PRESS
4805/24, Fourth Floor, Krishna House
Ansari Road, Daryaganj, New Delhi - 110002
Ph : 011-23282971, 45795759
E-mail : generalpressindia@gmail.com

www.generalpress.in

First Edition : 2020

ISBN : 9789389716412

Published by Azeem Ahmad Khan for General Press

Contents

Disclaimer

This book is a work of fiction. Any resemblance of characters or events to living or dead, or real incidents is purely coincidental. This work is solely presented for moral educational and motivational purposes to encourage young readers. The stories are inspired by real life events. Some events have been taken from biographical stories, which are already in public domain.

God's Return Gift

Mr. Roky had been diligently working as a motor mechanic for many years. His credibility was unquestionable. On the other hand was the service station's manager, Mr. Jokey, who was highly unscrupulous. Whenever the air conditioner of a car stopped working due to a minor issue, Roky was asked to raise an enormous bill to get it replaced. The manager was habitual of embezzling large amounts, which went unnoticed by the owner of the service station. Roky was later dismissed for standing against the deceit. He was a possessor of great moral conduct.

Roky was financially weak. He would provide for his family, whatever little he could from his meager earnings.

A calamity does not befall on anyone with prior notice and that is exactly what happened with Roky. His wife fell seriously ill and needed immediate medical aid. Roky with his itsy-bitsy savings, could hardly bear the expense of a private healthcare clinic, so instead, he decided on seeing a local doctor. The doctor prescribed medicines to Roky's wife and instructed for routine check-ups.

Roky set-up a roadside motor assistance, just so he could pay for his wife's medical needs. He worked painstakingly and could only earn a little on a day to day basis. He was undergoing an extreme financial crisis. His wife's condition aggravated with time.

One day, a heavy downpour made it difficult for him to get any customers. He was in dire need of money, but there was rarely any car seen passing by. His heart started palpitating heavily as the evening appeared. Everything seemed to be going wrong. He silently prayed and hoped for some customers to arrive and waited anxiously for some miracle to happen. When nothing happened after long hours of waiting, he started to lose hope, then wrapped up and headed back home.

He rushed home feeling confused and dejected. His legs trembled and refused to keep pace with his gait. On his way, he saw an elite class lady with an immensely luxurious car. She looked exhausted as she tried to open the boot of her car. She was in an urgent need of some help. Roky became overwhelmed with joy as he finally found a customer! He trotted fast and pulled up in front of her car.

The lady was frightened at the sight of a shabbily clad man and began wondering whether he was a robber. Roky had a pleasant smile on his face but the lady was agitated. She was keen on the idea that the man must have come with some evil intentions. She did not feel safe. Roky sensed the fear of the elegant looking lady.

Roky uttered in a respectful manner, "Madam, I am here to help you. I would suggest that you sit inside the car by the time I fix the flat tire." He then went ahead and introduced himself politely. Without further delay, he immediately crawled under the car and fixed the jack after great effort since the area was covered with mud puddles. He was completely soaked in dirt when the lady opened the car window and started to give Roky a brief introduction about herself. She told him that she was from the UK. Bewildered with the odd circumstances, she couldn't thank him enough for helping her.

Finally, the lady asked regarding the amount she owed him. She had already imagined all the horrible things that could have happened had Roky not helped her.

Roky hardly earned anything and badly needed some money. A thought struck Roky and he began thinking to himself, "this lady was not a customer but was a susceptible person in need of help. It is a human obligation to help the ones in need. God always helps those who help others." He was firm that God will surely ease his sufferings.

Roky told her, "Madam, I would like you to do something if you really want to pay me back. Whenever you see someone in need of help, help them with whatever you are capable of, that would indeed be my true payment." The lady was left mesmerized by the strength of Roky's virtuous character. He then waited till the lady drove off.

Even though the day was extremely tough, Roky felt a sense of achievement as he returned back home. He was later overcome by the worries of his household. He started thinking about how he could make a lot of money from the rich lady. But it was just a passing thought. He was at peace in realising that he made the correct decision by helping the lady in need. These days people sparingly care for humanity. They put all of their efforts in hope of getting more and more. Selflessness has become a rare virtue these days. It takes great courage to go out of your way to help someone in need, it is a task performed by great humans only. He then begged God to help him in return for whatever good he did.

The lady was filled with gratitude at receiving help in such a terrible situation. "Anything could have happened had God not sent Roky," she thought to herself. The lady was looking to grab something on her way as she was starving. A few miles down the road, she found a roadside food stall. She immediately got out of her car and began looking around. She was surrounded by a slum locality. The whole scene was unfamiliar to her. She realised, her stomach was brawling with pain. She needed something to eat immediately.

While she was looking around, a young boy appeared and greeted the lady amicably, then proceeded to receive her order. When he realized that the lady was completely drenched from head to toe, he hurriedly arranged a fresh towel and showed her the way to the nearest washroom. The boy stood waiting for the lady at the table.

The boy was the youngest worker at the food stall and would work really hard. The lady noticed how the young boy demonstrated resilience as he kept going with a smile on his face. She wondered, how can someone who was already suffering could be so kind and big hearted. She recalled the example of Roky.

The lady was in awe at the beauty of human conduct demonstrated by these two. After the lady finished her meal, the boy was paid with a hundred sterling pound bill. The boy quickly went to get change for her hundred pounds and came back to adjust the payment. But she was gone by the time the boy came back. He started looking for her but couldn't find her. He then went back to his work. While he was cleaning the table, he noticed a business card on the table attached with a slip of paper. It was written on the slip—

> *"You need not worry about the change, you don't owe me anything. Before I came here, somebody helped me with a smile and taught me how to help others. Now this was my chance. If you really want to pay me back, continue helping others in need with whatever you are capable of and God will give you back from unimaginable sources."*

Under the table napkin, he found five more bills of £100.

The boy was left astonished! He wondered how the lady could have possibly known how much money was needed by his parents. His mother suffered from acute illness and his father, Mr. Roky was sacked by his employer.

The young boy was well aware about the hardships his parents went through and the endless effort of his father to make ends meet. He then placed bills of £100 near his father's pillow and whispered softly, "Everything is going to be alright Dad."

The next morning, Roky was filled with joy. He had refused to accept money from the lady in need of help and now God had granted him a big compensation. His heart was filled with gratitude.

"When you do good, good will come back to you in unimaginable ways."

We should strive to treat others the same way we would want to be treated. Sooner or later, we will reap the fruits of our deeds; good or bad.

2

Honesty is a Rich Legacy

We are living in a world where wrongdoings have become universal and righteousness is almost an extinct attribute. Morality is more likely to change according to the circumstances of an individual. However, there are people who stand firm on their grounds and refuse to give away their uprightness for temporary benefits. Such people demonstrate great strength of character even though they are the ones who undergo several hardships and are least appreciated.

One such man was Mr. Harry, who was a trustworthy Government Officer. He was made to feel low for choosing to dress in a simplistic way, wearing an old-fashioned wristwatch and spectacles. Harry used to disregard their attitude and never once attempted to change his ideals to please the people around him.

Harry had a small and loving family. His wife Sudha was an efficient homemaker and a religiously committed individual. His only son Rakesh, was a distinguished 10th grade student in a world-class school. Each month, Harry had to undergo great financial difficulty in paying the educational expenses of his Rakesh. Harry wanted Rakesh to achieve great success and honor in life.

Rakesh was well aware of Harry's nature to never let go of moral principles, come what may. He was never extravagant like other officers. He would commute to the office on his old scooter or use public convenience.

Rakesh used to manage with whatever little had been provided by his father. Rakesh was praised by his teachers for being an outstanding student but his batchmates always distanced themselves from him. Rakesh was mocked by his classmates. He traveled to school on his old bicycle, while his batchmates had lavish bikes and cars. They had a blissful lifestyle.

Rakesh felt pathetic when he compared his own lifestyle with that of his batchmates. He lived in a rented apartment. Every other month, they had to face the harsh tongue of their landlord for not being able pay the rent on time. The condition of the water and electricity supply was miserable. He had a single school uniform which was worned out. He could tell that the other officers working with his father were living a lavish life. They were quite well off and enjoyed every amenity of life. Rakesh made a judgement without making an effort to see across the surface of the seemingly significant lifestyle and overcame with anger over the honesty of his father. He wanted him to be a "practical" man like his colleagues and earn enough by hook or crook so that he may also enjoy an effortless life like that of his friends. But his father's principle of being honest was a big barrier between his wishes.

One afternoon, on his way back home from school, Rakesh was engrossed in thinking about what his father's beliefs had served him so far in his life. He reached home and found his father battling for some final moments in life; he immediately called Rakesh to advise him to abide by the principle of honesty in life. He said to his son, "An honest person can be put to inconvenience, but the dishonest one is more likely to suffer in the long run."

Rakesh completely disregarded the situation, and his anger took the best of him in those moments. He said to his father in rage, "Papa, it is unfortunate you are dying without a penny in your bank. Your colleagues, whom you have tagged of being corrupt, have bulky bank balances and properties. What have you left for me? Even this apartment is rented. I have never received a blessing in my entire life! I shall never follow your principle of living a life of honesty!" Poor Harry was in immense pain as he left this world.

Years passed by and Rakesh had completed his education. He was at an interview in a multinational company. During the interview, the Chairman of the Interview Committee asked Rakesh about his father. Rakesh replied, "Sir, my father, Mr. Harry was a Government Officer. Sadly he is no longer with us." The Chairman in an utter surprise replied, "My goodness! Are you the son of Mr. Harry?"

He turned to the other members of the Interview Committee and said, "This man named Harry was the one who helped me when all my relatives turned their back on me. He was a stranger to me, but he verified my credentials in the capacity of being a Government Officer. Because of his verification and recommendation, I reached where I am today. He did everything without asking for anything in return. He didn't know me personally. He just offered help to a candidate in need."

He then turned to Rakesh and said, "I do not have any further questions for you, consider yourself as selected for this job, come tomorrow and collect your letter of appointment." Rakesh was in a state of complete disbelief of what had just happened. All these years, he had been thinking ill of his father and all it took was a stranger to finally make him realise the goodness his father possessed.

Later on, Rakesh became the Corporate Affairs Manager of the company. He received a car along with a driver, a well furnished house and a pretty huge monthly income including the additional perks. The Head Quarter of his company was in the UK and had to pay frequent visits to the UK. He worked hard and did his best to bring good results for the company.

After five years of his successful career, one day he got a call from a business tycoon who offered him a great job in the Industrial Estate provided he shares with him some secret information of the company he was engaged with. He was also lured a hefty cash reward beyond his imagination. Rakesh had been working hard with honesty for the last five years in the company. Everyone respected him and paid him high respect. How can he deceive his hard-earned respect? He made a firm decision to reject the offer. He chose not to deceive his company and instead continue to work as an honest, dignified employee.

During the Annual meeting of the company, the Managing Director announced his intention to resign and needed a competent and capable individual who could replace him. A personality with high integrity was sought. The matter was referred to the company's consultant, who submitted a report of five individuals who could have been suitable for the post. Resultantly, an interview was fixed to select the future Managing Director of the company.

The other day, Rakesh received a call, where he was asked to be present before the interview board that would take place in the Head Quarter of the company. During the interview, he was asked the secret of his success. He replied with utmost emotions, "My father paved these ways for me. It was long after he passed away, that I realised, he may have been financially incapable but he was truly rich in integrity, discipline and honesty."

The Chairman asked him, "Why did it take you so long to realise this fact?" He told him, "All this while,

I used to think that being an honest person can only bring pain and suffering in life. I disrespected my father for advising me to live a life based on the principle of honesty. When I walked in for the interview, unprepared, having no faith in my capabilities and got selected based on the integrity of my father, then I realised that people truly honour you for your goodness." He was then asked, "Will you follow your father's last advice?

Rakesh kept silent for a long time unable to utter anything. He remembered his father in those moments and asked God to forgive him for treating him badly. He replied with utmost confidence, "Yes Sir, now that I have realised the role values play in our life, I shall forever abide by the principle of honesty in all my dealings."

The interviewer responded, "Mr. Rakesh, we all know, you have now accepted the sound principle of honesty like your father. The offer of a high rise in the Industrial Estate and cash reward was planned by us to test your honesty. Our organization planted the offer of the Industrial Estate. You have successfully passed that test." Rakesh realised that the reward for being honest comes slowly but surely.

Integrity, discipline, self-control makes a man rich in its true sense and not the bank balances.

"No legacy is as rich as honesty. We might face certain problems for some time, but it will all be worth it in the end. We will forever live with peace of mind."

Good Habits

My name is Ankit and now I have reached the age where I have started thinking about living an independent life. Having belonged to a middle-class family, I face several problems; be it financial or otherwise. My father is a small shopkeeper, who earns a meager income. My mother is a home-maker and a religiously committed woman. With her hard work, she perfectly manages the household with the limited available resources and tries her level best to save money wherever possible. Being cautious about money, my parents keep a strict eye on the spending habits of all family members.

I am worried about the hardships that my parents undergo on a daily basis and want to improve the financial condition of the family. For the same reason, I am desperately looking for a job and investing a good amount of time in preparing for it.

It was a hot summer day and the Sun was at its peak. I was busy making preparations for my job interview. I was not only bothered by the hot weather but more by my father, who was constantly worried about the electricity bill. He would call me every now and then, and ask me to switch off the lights. Early in the morning, my mom would start her soliloquy without caring for anyone or anything. I was not all happy with these unreasonable and rigid rules imposed by my parents to ensure minimum wastage of resources.

My parents have been worried about the marriage of my sister, who has crossed her 30s. Every marriage proposal comes with a list of demands for expensive items.

We at least need a minimum of ten lac rupees for her marriage. Because of this family issue, my parents are becoming more miser each passing day. I am looking for a way out to these problems.

Finally the day I was looking forward to has arrived! It was the day of my interview. I hurried to reach my interview destination on time. While I was leaving the house, I thought to myself, "If I get selected today, I will take the responsibility for my sister's wedding." My parents are living under the social pressure for delaying her marriage. If I get selected for the post, I will leave no stone unturned to make my sister and my parents happy. It will also stop the daily squabbling and bickering of my parents and hopefully it will also restore the lost peace in our home.

Whenever I wake up in the morning, a roaring sound comes, "fold your blanket and keep it in the storeroom!" I am not allowed to switch on the lights in the bathroom. I have to keep the light off while taking a shower. It is the strict instruction of my father. Immediately after coming out of the bathroom, I hear my mom saying, "Put the towel in the right place or it will be thrown out!"

It is too much to stand right from the start of the morning. This is a mandatory part of my everyday routine. In other words, they keep me jumping now and then.

Just before I step out of the house, my mother reconfirms whether the extra lights and fans were switched off properly or if the clothes were placed in the laundry basket. All these are constant reminders whenever I move out.

I pray that God grants me this job, so I can get away with these problems. When I reached the interview destination, I found many candidates walking in. The interview was scheduled for 10 a.m. It's already ten o'clock and the lights of the office veranda are still on. Not one but there are many bulbs still waiting for someone to switch them off. I recollected the advice of my father and kept my bag aside and switched off all the lights that were on unnecessarily. During day time no extra light is required.

When I headed to the washroom, I saw water dripping from the tap. It was a clear wastage of precious water. I remember the scolding of my mother and closed the water tap tight. As soon as I reached my place, I was confused to see no candidate was present. I checked the notice board and found that the interview was scheduled on the second floor. I picked up my bag and proceeded to the second floor.

I saw that some water was spilt on the stairs. Someone might have gotten slipped accidentally and could get seriously injured. I must do something. But there is nothing available to wipe the stair dry. I went to the nearby dustbin, picked up some used papers and wiped the stairs dry. It seemed as though everyone was careless in this office.

On the second floor, the interview already started. I immediately grabbed a seat and waited for my turn. The candidates present were called in and were sent out immediately. "How can a candidate be interviewed in such a short time? How come their files are examined so quickly?" I thought to myself.

When my turn came and I went inside, I placed my profile before the Interview Board and waited for the tricky questions that may be asked to me. The Chairman looked at the papers and seemed satisfied. But he also expressed that they were not only looking for a capable candidate but also a responsible one. I was about to lose hope in getting the job, but surprisingly enough, the interviewer glanced at my face with a smile and said, "When are you joining?" He told me that they were watching all the activities of the candidates right from the beginning on the CCTV. Every candidate came but nobody switched off the lights, no one turned off the running tap, and nobody wiped the wet stairs. He told me that I was the only one who cared for such little things that matter most in life.

He then went ahead and asked me, "Is this your natural habit or did someone train you?" At this I responded, "No Sir, I learned this all under compulsion." "What compulsion? What do you mean by compulsion?" he asked in a firm tone. "Sir, the credit goes to my parents, who every now and then used to guide me to care of the resources and use them wisely.

But sir, I also acknowledge that I would get quite irritated by their constant reminders." "You are blessed to have such parents who taught you the value of life.", he responded.

At that moment, I felt regret for not appreciating my parents enough. I took their advice in a negative way. They were in fact fulfilling the responsibility of being good parents. I realised that often times we forget that they are our well-wishers.

That day I took an oath to listen to every single advice of my parents and adhere to it with full devotion as it will only going to benefit me in the long run.

Who is Richer than a Rich Man?

(Story of Bill Gates)

Soham, a class 10th student, lived in a poor family. He wished if his parents were wealthy, he could have enjoyed life like a rich man. He had a blank picture of rich people in his mind. For him being rich means having the freedom to do just as you like – to work at a job you love without having to worry about how much it pays, or to give up work completely to pursue some other interest without wanting to earn a living from it. He decided to become a rich man. Pursuing his devotion he started to collect maximum information about rich persons. When he found out that Mr. Bill Gates is the richest person in the world. He concentrated his full attention searching about the lifestyle of this richest person in the world.

After reading his biography he came to know that Bill Gates was born on the 28th of October, 1955 with a silver spoon in his mouth. While his father was a lawyer, his grandfather was the President of the National Bank. Since childhood, he had a passion for computers and wanted to become a millionaire by starting his own company.

Driven by his intense interest in computers, he met a boy named Paul Allen with a similar interest in computers. Both joined hands and after their studies, they started a business together. Facing many teething troubles both of them started one software company that was registered with the name of Microsoft in 1975.

It was in the year of 1986 after eleven years of hard work, that Bill Gates invented software called Microsoft Windows. With a great vision and hard work, Bill Gates took Microsoft to become the world's number one software company. His vision and hard work made him the world's richest man as well.

Bill Gates was named the richest man in the world by Forbes' annual list of the world's billionaires. This was the 16th time that the founder of Microsoft claimed the top spot. He emerged as an incredible man who created a software empire and became the richest man in the world.

Soham was greatly inspired after reading his biography as he was also interested in computers. He now started reading the further story of Bill Gates with more interest. While reading his biography with many divergent details, he happened to come across a very interesting story about him.

Once many years ago because of a squabble over some matter with management, he was facing dismissal. It was an occasion for him to spend some time with his old friends, he was missing for a long time.

These friends were delighted to sit in close proximity to the richest man in the world. Out of curiosity one of them asked Bill Gates, "Is there anyone richer than you?"

"Yes, there is one man who is richer than me."

"Who is that man?" The next question came instantly.

"I do not remember his name but I recollect that I had gone to New York Airport. Before checking in for boarding I was just looking at daily newspapers and magazines. I wanted to purchase one newspaper and picked up one copy to buy. As soon as I put my hands in my pocket, I found no small coins available with me. With a heavy heart, I kept the newspaper back and stood up to leave the place. The expressions on my face were observed by the vendor. When he saw my interest and my desire to purchase the newspaper, he called me and told me this newspaper is for you. I watched carefully this black boy who was offering me the desired newspaper. In a perplexing situation, I hesitated to accept his offer having no change money, though I was very keen to read it. I felt low; neither was I able to buy the paper nor was willing to refuse the offer. I stood silent just watching the black boy. It was not possible for me to decide what to do. Should I accept the offer or refuse it? It was not possible for me to resist the temptation of the newspaper but without money, I was not able to accept it either. With a heavy heart, I said, 'but I don't have change money.' He smiled and said, 'No problem, I would like to give you for free.' I took the newspaper and left with thanks."

After this Bill Gates paused for a moment to see the reaction of his friends who were listening to his story. After a while he continued, "You know I remain busy all the time during day and night and don't get time to spare some moments over petty matters. The incident went out of my mind."

He continued, "When I happened to visit the same Airport again after three months, then as per my habit, I was again looking for the Newspapers and magazines put up for sale. I started searching for some coins in my pocket and found nothing. The same boy observed my intention and without asking anything he offered me the desired paper once again. He said, 'it is for you, free of cost.' It was a moment of joy for me to find such a compassionate boy willing to offer free of cost to bring a smile on the face of unknown people."

He said, "My curiosity increased and I asked the boy, 'Dear friend three months ago, you gave one newspaper free of cost and today also you are offering it for free. Do you deal with everyone who comes across you in this situation?'"

The boy responded, "No, not to everyone, but when I feel the customer's intense desire, and his willingness to pay but because of certain reasons they are unable to pay, I offer them out of my profit amount. I don't want to see someone get disheartened just for little money."

Bill Gates continued, "His words and kind gestures stayed in my mind and I was thinking on what basis and what sagacity this was possible."

The poor black boy, already discarded by the society of white people, was so generous that he offered his sale item free of cost to a well-clad white person only because they were interested in buying it but were not able to pay for some reasons.

This episode touched the heart of little young chap Sohan while reading the biography of Bill Gates. How a poor boy could afford to lose his hard earned money to serve the purpose of a needy man was a big question haunting his mind. He started to read further with more interest.

Bill Gates continued answering the question, "Is there anyone richer than you?" and said:

"After 19 years when I reached the height of my destiny, I decided to find this person to bring back his beauty and compensate him. I formed a team and told them to go to the airport and inform me about the black boy who was selling the newspapers. After a month and a half of research and investigation, they found out that the black boy is currently a theater keeper."

Bill Gates reached there and asked him, "Do you know me?"

The man said, "Yes, I know you well. You are famous Bill Gates, the acclaimed richest person in the world."

Mr Gates responded, "Very good, your memory is very sharp that you remember me," Bill Gates said. "Well, you may also remember giving me a free newspaper two times many years ago?"

Man replied, "Yes, I do not forget easily. I remember it very well."

"Okay, it is good you still remember me. Let us be good friends. Now, I want to compensate you for your kindness. I am going to give you everything that you want." Mr Gates responded.

The black young man replied, "You can't compensate me."

Mr Gates said, "Why?" He replied, "Because, I gave you when I was poor and you want to give me when you are rich. So how do you compensate for it?"

Mr Gates said, "I think that the black young man is richer than me."

You don't have to have money in order to help others.

A wise man once said, "Money and wealth are an element of vanity. When you die, all possessions go to someone else. What stays is the legacy of good that you leave behind. "

Our Ex-President APJ Abdul Kalam rightly said, "Don't make more money, make more friends."

High Moral Character

(Story of Lal Bahadur Shastri)

There is a famous saying, “Power tends to corrupt, and absolute power corrupts absolutely.” Political leaders use their power to get things done. Some exceptional leaders use it for the welfare of other people while most leaders use it for personal gains. Resultantly in many cases, elected leaders get intoxicated by power and misuse it as they wish. In their mind, negative use of power prevails upon its positive use. But nonetheless, there is an inspiring example of a top political leader, who later became the Prime Minister of India.

During a debate of students in a school where the teacher was explaining, how difficult it can be to adhere to sound principles of high morals when you are in the state of authority and power. He explained when most people after gaining power succumb to corruption how a simple man belonging to a poor family was firm and determined to keep his morals high even after retaining the top most power in a country where many others succumb to the disease of corruption.

The teacher said, "You might have heard about the name of Lal Bahadur Shastri Ji who became the second Prime Minister of India. After the death of first Prime Minister Jawaharlal Nehru Ji a type of vacuum was created in the Indian politics. Every Indian was watching with crossed fingers for a person who could lead India efficiently like Jawaharlal Nehru. Two people were suitable for the post. One was Morarji Desai and the other was Lal Bahadur Shastri. Morarji Desai was a senior, more experienced, able and honest leader. On the other hand Lal Bahadur Shastri was a person who belonged to a poor family, lived a simple life and was also a junior. But in spite of all this he was more flexible, highly ethical and down to earth. He became the most favorite of all, which made him win over Morarji Desai, and he proved to be the right choice.

His father Sharda Prasad Shrivastava was a school teacher who passed away when he was barely two years old. His mother Ramdulari Devi went to live with her father Hazari Lal's house with her children. In his maternal house, Lal Bahadur Shastri acquired virtues like boldness, love for all, patience, self-control, courtesy, and selflessness from childhood. He grew up with a high moral ethics. He was against the prevailing caste system and therefore dropped his surname "Shrivastava". The title "Shastri" was given after the completion of his graduation at Kashi Vidyapeeth. He was widely known for his ethics and morality.

When he became the Railway minister, his mother asked him about his job. Shastri *Ji* did not inform her about his ministerial position and simply said, "I am working with Railway." Once the Railway Ministry organized a function where he was invited as a chief guest in his capacity as Railway Minister. He informed his mother about the function and its venue before leaving the house. Mother was curious to know about his job. She wanted to know where his son is working. After some time his mother also reached the venue. Because of the presence of the minister, the security was on high alert. No one was allowed to enter the venue without verification of antecedents.

His mother was stopped at the gate by the security officer for inquiry. She informed the security that her son is working with the railway and that she was there to meet him."

"What is the name of your son?" the security officer asked. When she told the name, no one could believe her. How can a simply clad, ordinary woman be the mother of the railway minister? Suspicion aroused in the mind of the security officer. He assumed that the lady was lying. 'How can she be the mother of a Cabinet Minister?' She has come here all alone without any security. She can never be the mother of a minister', he thought.

The security officer was confused if he permits entry and later the lady proves to be a deceit, he may lose his job. In case her entry is refused and she happens to be the mother of minister he may lose his job either way. The security officer was caught in a catch 22 situation. Neither was he able to permit her nor to refuse. The ultimate decision was taken to inform the minister about this lady and her claim.

Senior security officer went to Lal Bahadur Shastri and informed him that a woman is standing at the gate and is insisting on meeting you. She claims her to be your mother. Lal Bahadur Shastri was a short stature person as such was not able to see the woman in a place crowded by hundreds of people. He decided to go to the gate and see the woman himself.

On seeing his mother at the gate he touched her feet and took her along with him and offered a comfortable seat near him. He publicly announced how his mother loved him that she reached here all alone to see him.

It was time for him to give the inaugural speech but he kept mum and spent his time talking with his mother. After some time he sent his mother home. After the function was over there was a press conference of Railway Minister Lal Bahadur Shastri.

The first question that came from a prominent journalist was astonishing.

"Sir, your mother was here sitting with you. Why did you avoid addressing the public in her presence?"

Shastri Ji responded, "Please don't be curious. There is nothing for me to hide from you. I didn't deliver my speech in her presence because I lied before her. I have not informed her that I am the Minister of Railway. I simply told her that I am working in the railway ministry. That is why I avoided addressing the public in her presence."

He continued, "My mother does not know that I am a minister. She is a very simple, social and homely lady. If she knows about my actual position, she will start recommending people which I shall not be able to refuse. I cannot refuse anything to my mother. In such circumstances, she may probably become arrogant, which I don't want. Neither I can refuse my mother nor I can accept undue recommendations. Hearing the answer everyone was stunned."

It is rare to find people of such high morals.

Lal Bahadur Shastri was awarded the Bharat Ratna, India's highest civilian award posthumously in 1966.

One should never let power and authority corrupt intellect and morals. True power and authority should make a person humble and one should use it to prevail ultimate justice.

Abundance of Gratitude

I am Jonathan Petti. I love to walk down the memory lane whenever I miss my mother. A lot happened during my childhood that has shaped my life.

I was about ten when my mother passed away. Despite her ill-health, she was concerned about all of us.

One day, she suffered from a severe heart attack and left for her heavenly abode without giving us any chance of taking her to the hospital. I, my elder brother and my father all were dependent on her. She was the one who devoted her entire life just to see us happy. Her happiness lied in seeing us happy. She was sad if any one of us was in trouble.

After her death, for about ten days we lived like orphans but my father soon rose to the occasion and played the duty of both father and that of a mother. He started looking after both of us. He was particular about our health, study, diet, and upkeep of the house like our mother. He was now less a father and more a mother. From the very beginning we both brothers were careless, undisciplined and naughty under the aegis of the loving mother. Being old aged it was now difficult for our father to cope up with the given situations.

Now was the time that made us a silent spectator of things to happen. We had hundreds of complaints with our mother, dinner is not good, you do not play with us, our lunch boxes are not tasty, and our uniform is dirty. Mother always smiled and did what we wanted.

In his old age, our father devoted his full attention to keep us happy and see us behaving in a normal way. When it became difficult for him to play the dual role of father and that of a mother he appointed an assistant who would look after both of us.

She was a widow but very sweet by nature. Initially, we were not happy with her but as time passed, she won our hearts with her love and affection. As our mother, she was very particular about our health and safety. She would get up early in the morning, to serve us the bed tea, prepare for our bath, iron our dresses, polish the shoes and a neat handkerchief was placed with a nicely packed lunch box. We brothers could not believe whether the food was cooked by our mother or by our assistant. It was truly sumptuous.

The time passed and my elder brother went to the USA for his post-graduation. I was still in my school. I started feeling alone in the absence of my brother. Old memories haunted my mind now and then. I left interest in the study, sports and stopped watching TV. My father got worried about my health. He decided to send me to a hostel. My elder brother was in the USA and I was admitted to a hostel. My father had done his best to get me admitted to a famous college for Law Degree and paid through his nose to bear the heavy cost towards my study and hostel charges. But I always remained uncomfortable.

I faced many difficulties and hurdles such as home-made food, adjustment issues, personal helplessness, distress, changes in eating and sleeping habits and many other issues.

Every coin has a flip side, and no exception exists for the life you live at home and the life you live in a hostel. We have to bear the side of the coin that is up for us. Recollecting old memories, I remember while in school I always waited for the sumptuous food prepared by our mother. I was dying to eat homemade food. Fed up from hostel food I decided to visit home. I earnestly was longing for homemade food and a loving environment of our home.

I suddenly decided to reach home from my hostel without informing anybody. The first thing my mother was meticulous was to cook the food immediately on reaching home after school. The day when I reached home from the hostel, my father opened the door. He was filled with joy to see me unexpectedly. Not knowing what to do, he instantly remembered my mother and entered the kitchen to cook something for me. The assistant was watching the love and affection of a father for his son. She was eager to cook good food for me but because of the intense desire of my father, she remained a silent spectator.

After keeping food on the dining table father invited me and sat beside me watching me eat my meal. Everything prepared by his magical hands was full of divine taste. I silently finished eating and started washing dishes. Father was still looking at me.

Now our assistant came forward and took the plate from my hands and placed it in the dish-washer. Holding, my hand she dragged me to sit on a sofa and sat beside me.

"I know you have not liked the food. I am sorry, I allowed your father to cook for you. It is his eternal love for you." she said.

I stood still and motionless when I heard her words and said, "What do you mean? My Papa is a good cook, the food was great and delicious. I enjoyed it. I love him."

She said, "Don't tell a lie, what you say is not clear from your expression."

I told her, "No, it's true. I enjoy it bit by bit that dissolves unique taste in my mouth. The aroma of spices used by him increases my appetite. I praise his cooking among all my friends."

"Really? Do you praise his cooking among your friends?" The assistant said in a slanting way.

I responded, "I swear, I do praise his cooking."

Then she asked, "And what about my cooking?"

I responded, "You cook so well, I end up overeating."

She looked at my face with surprise and after a while said, "You always eat in a hurry, never saying anything. You never told your father or to me, you like our cooking, so I thought you eat in a hurry because you do not enjoy it."

I told her, "It is true I eat in a hurry because I cannot resist the temptation of finishing such a delicious food quickly."

"Then you should have appreciated your father and me," she said.

She said something really profound, "Remember one thing, whenever someone does a nice thing for you, you should express your gratitude and thank that person. If you don't express it, then he might think you dislike his actions and he may stop doing those nice things for anybody."

Her words created a ray of perspicacity for me. Her words of wisdom touched my heart. From that day onward, I thanked everyone for literally everything. If someone did something for me but it didn't help me, even then I would thank that person profusely. Later it became my habit. I cannot think when my habit of thanking others became a Magic Wand for me.

The magic started happening in my life.

People liked me more. They talked to me more, shared with me, and were friendlier. I was happier than ever. My teachers, friends, relatives, and people now loved me more. After completing the hostel, when I went home after attending farewell of the last day of my hostel I found a bundle of cards with best wishes. "Thanks, dad and assistant," I said instinctively.

Father and assistant both smiled and said, "We have not arranged all these cards for you. These all are from your classmates, teachers and other employees of the hostel. They found you to be the best student who understands the value of others and reciprocates being thankful to all of them."

These two simple words of "THANK YOU" made a huge difference that people who disliked my being unthankful now have great appreciation for me.

That is the power of appreciation. When you have it, all is right in the world, but when it is missing life is empty. Dad further told me that, "People who practice gratitude experience fewer aches and pains. Sleep better, have higher rates of resilience, experience increased self-esteem, experience increased immunity and happiness, increased energy, optimism, and empathy.

When gratitude resides in your life as a leading core value, it gives you the power to rest in any situation with grace, dignity, and hope.

It is easy to say thank you for all the easy moments. But only those who thank the hardships will enjoy a truly satisfying life. Gratitude has the power to turn negative into positive."

Accept Challenges

Sumit and Amit two friends studying in the same school joined NCC on the behest of their teacher. They were told that NCC stands for National Cadets Corps associated with Indian Military Cadet Corps. The organization of NCC frequently invites students from schools and colleges to develop them for Indian security in the future. For training, NCC camps are organized from time to time. Both friends were eager to serve the nation and joined NCC happily.

After two months of their joining NCC, a final camp was organized in a forest area primarily to create self-confidence in students. Sumit and Amit both were eager to attend the camp, so they joined it. After a few lessons in the classroom, they were required to start a track through the forest.

On the decided day, the Instructor asked both of them to come and meet him at the start of the track through the forest. Both of them reached there on decided time as disciplined candidates. There was a board showing the track routes from the start point to the endpoint. The Instructor pointed to the board and said, "You both have to start here and reach the endpoint of the track."

"The time taken by you completing the track will also affect the result of the test which will happen next week."

Both of them agreed to accept the challenge and sought the blessing of the Instructor. The instructor wished them good luck and started the race. Both of them started together running at great speed to complete the task in minimum possible time. After a while, they saw that the track was divided into two paths. It was also shown on the signboard that indicated one path as longer but easy and the second path as shorter but difficult. Both had to decide whether to choose an easy path or a difficult path.

Amit decided to follow a path that was clear and was easier to go through. On the contrary, Sumit decided to take the shorter path which was difficult. The path chosen by Sumit was blocked at many places either by fallen logs, wide trenches and many other hurdles. But it was definitely a shorter route to reach the endpoint of the track.

Amit was first to finish the track at the given time. The path chosen by him was simple clear with no blockage or other hurdles. He felt clever as he came first and passed the track easily avoiding all the obstacles and hindrances of the difficult path.

Sumit took some time to reach the endpoint. He had to pass through the path which was full of difficulties, obstacles, ditches and trenches. He had virtually been battling with the difficult track. When Sumit reached the endpoint of the track, Amit proudly said, "I am glad I chose the easier path as the difficult path might have delayed my race." Amit was jubilant over his success in the first round of the race. He patted his back and danced all around. Sumit stood silent watching his contentment. It was the first round of the race.

Next week both were asked to reach another location for the second round of the race. It was a place in the forest on the edge of a deep, narrow gorge with steep sides.

The instructor warned them about the risk involved and said, "You have to jump to the other side of this gorge."

The students were taken back as the distance was a few meters wide. Amit was disorientated to see the width of the gorge. He contemplated whether or not the risk should be taken. If successful, he will be the sole winner. He didn't think of being unsuccessful in the track rather thought of the consequences, what if he fell down the valley in his attempt to take the chance. He was more serious about the consequences of falling, if he failed to jump successfully. Perhaps, he may be injured seriously. He could not work up the courage and dropped the idea of completing the track. He, therefore, stepped back from the test.

Now the instructor looked at Sumit who was also in a serious mood. He remembered the track of his first test. He did not only jump over the big logs, deep ditches but he also jumped across a very wide gap there. He was hopeful now.

He watched the gorge carefully, took a deep breath. After measuring his run-up he dashed towards the gorge and launched himself into the air. It was hardly a pace of twinkle of an eye and he made it.

Other students had also taken this test. Few of them were successful but the majority of them failed to complete the test. The instructor explained to the students that the test was planned in two rounds. The first-round option was given to students to choose an easy path or a difficult one. The difficult path was made in such a way that completing it would have prepared them for the second round of tests. Those who chose an easy path were able to complete it only because it was an easy one. But they were not able to complete the second path which would have prepared them for tougher challenges.

Accepting your challenges opens the door to major breakthroughs, and the hidden opportunities surrounding them.

To run away from your problems without facing them is never the solution. Life is full of challenges. Time to time, we face smaller or bigger obstacles in our life. Most people run away from their problems and start looking for some easy way out. In the end, they are caught up with much bigger problems. If we choose to stay within our comfort zone all the time, we will never be able to grow. Growth requires strength and strength ultimately comes when we start working on our skills and take up challenges.

Value of Money

There lived a businessman in a village. He was known for his honesty and hard work. The people living in the village had great respect for him. He was always ready to help villagers during their difficult days. He worked hard day and night to establish his business and faced many hurdles. Even when the society criticized him, he remained benevolent by heart.

He had a son, whom he wanted to work hard and earn money through honest means. He wished his son should earn a good reputation like him and enjoy a well-established status in society. But contrary to his wishes and expectations, his son was caught in the company of wrong people, which had a negative influence on him.

He started developing bad habits also. Whenever his father wanted his help for the business, he had a list of excuses ready in order to avoid giving him any kind of help. He was proud of his father only he had a lot of money. Instead of helping his father, he loved to roam around with his stray friends throughout the day. He was in the habit of spending huge amounts of money to entertain his toady friends just for showing his upper hand. The moment any friend showed him any kind of disrespect, he immediately started behaving bossy. He was quick to physically abuse others. At home, he was whining from the moment he woke up.

As he grew in the habit of spending money, he started wasting money like water at the behest of his friends.

The behavior and activities of son became a big cause of concern for his father. He was worried to see his hard-earned money go to waste by his spoiled son. He expected his son would grow up to take charge of his business and that he would then be free to go on a pilgrimage with his wife.

The man was disheartened with the growing bad habits of his son. He was very annoyed also. One day he called his son and rebuked him for his spending habits. He wanted him to learn how difficult it is to earn money with honesty and hard work. He stopped giving him any money.

He commanded, "I want you to go out and earn one rupee by the evening. If you fail to earn one rupee you will not be allowed to live in my house nor you would get food."

The son never expected anything harsher than the punishment of earning money. He begged his father to withdraw his command but the father was adamant. He wanted his son to know the value of money. The son felt helpless after seeing this attitude of his father and started crying.

His mother was watching the entire drama from behind the doors. She was not able to bear the pain of her son. Her heart started palpitating. Watching her son cry bitterly, the mother became overwhelmed with love. Mother secretly gave a coin of one rupee to her son and asked him to go out of the house and return in the evening and, then give the coin to father as if it was earned by him after great labour.

Son was happy to get this money from his mother. He went out of the house to spend his day with his stray friends and came back in the evening. He was stopped at the gate and was prohibited entry into the house without showing the coin. Son searched his pockets and offered a coin of one rupee to his father.

They lived in a very big house. For water supply, there was a well built in the open ground of the house. Father asked him to throw the money in the well. He quickly obeyed the orders of his father and threw money in the well without any hesitation.

It became his daily practice. In this way, he would take money from his mother every day and would go to his father and then the father would ask him to throw the money in the well and he would obey his orders. The rich man was very clever and he sensed that something fishy was going on behind his back. He also knew his wife's profound love for her only son. He was suspicious of his wife that she might be helping their son. He found out the whole thing and sent his wife to her maternal house for a few days.

His son was finally trapped now. He kept thinking all day as he did not know what to do now. Since he never offered to help his father, he found it difficult to earn a single one rupee now. There was no solution other than to earn money as per the orders of his father. If he fails to earn money he will not be allowed to enter the house.

Now it was clear that he had to work hard and earn money. He searched for some petty jobs but without experience, he was denied a job everywhere. Eventually, he set out to find a work that of a porter. After spending two hours working on carrying a heavy load on his back like a porter he was able to get one rupee. He was so happy that he kissed the coin and kept it safely in his pocket. He arrived home to give money to his father wishing a big patting of good work on his ailing back. The father looked at the sweating boy and asked him to throw the coin in the well as before.

The boy was bewildered, he felt as if someone was pricking his body with a sharp object. It was painful for him. He remembered how hard he worked to earn that one rupee coin and now he is being asked to throw it in the well. This was totally unjustified.

Son replied to his father, "I have worked very hard today, my body is aching, I was sweating a lot to earn this money and now you want me to throw it in the well? Come what may, I can never throw it away." Son refused to obey the orders of his father and took the coin to keep it safely in the house.

As soon as these words came out of his mouth, father was happy to hear these words that he did not need anything more. His son understood the value of money and honesty. He became responsible and serious about his life.

We tend to take our blessings for granted. At times, struggles teach us lessons that ease wouldn't. When we go through struggles in life, that is when we truly appreciate and value our blessings.

9

Value of a Man

There lived a carpenter in a remote village in India. His name was Kalu Ram but he was called Kaku. He was an expert artisan in the profession of woodcraft. He used to make extraordinary pieces of carved wood, which was liked far and wide by people. He had a huge stock of good quality wood.

His son, Rahul was a student of 10th class. He had a sharp mind but was also a notorious student. His teachers were fed up with his long list of tricky questions. Now and then he would ask such questions that would have never crossed the minds of other students. Being a voracious reader he used to read truth-seeking books.

Once he was sitting in his father's shop, watching everything his father made out of rough logs of wood. He was surprised to see one idol made of wood by his father. He liked it very much.

Rahul asked his father, "What does this idol cost?" Before the father could answer he asked another question, "What is the cost of this wooden frame? And what is the cost of this flowerpot?" His father Kaku was surprised about the series of questions asked by his son in a spiraling row.

Before he could manage to think about answers there was yet another question.

In his innocence, Rahul asked, "Father what is the value of a man?"

Father who was busy with his customers stopped his work and looked at the face of his son and was surprised to hear such a serious question from a young boy. Father asked him, "Why? Why are you asking this question?"

"See dad, everything in this world has some value. We judge most of the things by their value only. A man must also have some value. So I ask you, what is the value of a man?"

"Look son, the value of a human is priceless and it is not possible to judge the value of a man in monetary terms," Father said.

"But my teacher told me, all human beings are equally valuable and important. But when everything else has different values, then how can all humans be treated equally and equally important?" Son asked.

"Your teacher is right." Father replied.

Rahul was not able to understand what his teacher said and what now his father was telling.

Being unsatisfied the son further asked, "If all humans are equal then why is there any poor and rich in this world. Why is someone less privileged than others? Why is one man a servant and another is a master?"

Hearing these questions, the father kept silent for some time. He was finding it difficult to find a suitable answer. Had this question been asked by a mature person, father could have managed to explain the philosophy of being a human. But it was difficult to make a child understand deep-rooted theories which have been explained by people of wisdom. Finding no easy answer he thought of a trick and asked his son to bring a rough log of wood from the storeroom.

The boy immediately went into the storeroom and brought a rough log of wood.

Father watched the log carefully and asked the boy, "In your opinion what should be the cost of this piece of rough wood which you have brought from the storeroom?"

Son watched the piece of wood carefully. After examining the wood he said, "It is just rough wood and can be used for fire purposes only. As such it should not cost more than 200/- Rupees."

"Your idea is correct son. Being a piece of rough wood it should not cost more than two hundred rupees. But if I make walking sticks out of this wood and sell them for use by old people, how much would it cost?"

"Of course, its price shall increase as it includes the cost of efforts of carving and it would cost for about 1000 rupees."

"And if I make a Carved Pillar for use in a temple, what would it then cost?"

The boy was confused. Not able to make out the cost of a carved pillar for use in a temple, he started calculating on his fingers. After some serious thinking, he said, "And then it will cost a lot. Carving a pillar needs more effort to put in."

"Very good answer son, you are right! Now you understand that the cost of wood gets changed depending on the making and use?"

The father then explained to his son, "Similarly, the value of a man is not in what he is at the moment, but is determined by what he can make of himself with right efforts. If he is satisfied with his present position without putting in efforts for growth his value shall be negative. He will be a worthless man because he is not prepared to face the difficulties of life."

We have great expectations. We have set higher goals for our life. We wish to reach the top of the highest ladder of success but at the same time, we get disheartened looking at our present status. We start thinking of ourselves as worthless. We only develop negative views in our minds facing difficulties in life. We forget that God has gifted us immense power. We forget that life is always full of opportunities. Sometimes opportunities knock on our door but we refuse and do not open the door. Many times in our life the conditions are not good but these adverse conditions cannot reduce our inherent value of being a human. The only things we should always keep improving is ourselves, learn the best skills to increase our value like a log of wood that increased its value by becoming more useful.

Be Good to Others

Turn the pages of history and you will find a very long list of kings and monarchs who were very cruel to their subjects. They had terrible methods to punish alleged transgressors, villains, enemies and anyone else who was unlucky enough to be in the wrong place at the wrong time. Their ways of punishment included crucifixion, burning alive, stoning, boiling in water or oil, crushing by elephants, and all kinds of other possible torture.

In present times also there are examples of extreme ways of giving torturous punishments. The existing president of North Korean dictator Kim Jung-Un killed his uncles Jang Sung Taek and his assistants to starving dogs. Jung and his assistants had been executed via a process known as *quan jue* (i.e. execution by dogs) in which he and five of his aides were stripped naked and thrown into a cage with 120 dogs that were kept starved for three days. The famished dogs then proceeded to tear apart and then devour Jang and his aides in an hour-long process that was personally supervised by Kim Jung-Un and witnessed by 300 senior officials.

It is an example of the extreme brutality of the North Korean Regime. At the time of execution Jang was vice-chairman of North Korea and the fault was that he was politically motivated for self raise and was anti-party.

When the world is full of malevolent people, it is difficult to find someone considerate. Here is a story that will teach us how being good pays us in the long run, even when it is with animals.

There was once a king, who was very cruel and unjust. He was so cruel that he used new ways of torturing innocent people just for his entertainment. Once he was out to inspect his territory and saw a man who did not stand up and bowed his head in respect of the king. It was the law that every citizen was supposed to stand up and bow his head in respect of the king as he passed by him. This man disobeyed his rule and was subjected to severe punishment. Stripped naked and tied with ropes he was hanged on huge flames till his body was completely burnt. The cruel king sat before the fire with his officials and family members and enjoyed the event as if it was some kind of a play. Later, it was found that the victim of the ultimate cruelty was a blind man. The innocent person was crucified for no fault of his.

The king was so cruel that his subjects yearned for his death or dethronement.

One day, he commanded all his subjects to be present in the assembly hall for an important announcement.

All citizens were in a dilemma thinking something wrong was going to happen with them. To their utter surprise, the cruel king announced to all citizens, "I have decided to turn over a new leaf. From now onwards, there shall be no more cruelty, no more injustice," he promised.

Nobody was able to digest what the king announced. Suspicious over his announcement no one could place any trust with him. But the king proved as good as his words. He started behaving very gently. He even ignored the mistake of people that was earlier enough to be considered for a death sentence. Everyone was surprised by the suddenly changed behavior of their king. It became a matter of gossip for everyone. Everybody was curious to know the secret behind his being a benevolent king. Cruelty was a matter of joy for him and he enjoyed experimenting new methods of cruelty to punish even innocent people.

Time passed and people were still living in suspicion. After months of his transformation, one of his ministers pulled up enough courage to ask him as to what had brought about change in his heart.

Nobody so far could dare ask any question to the king. How dare this minister was here to question his decision? King looked at the minister with his staring eyes. Minister was frightened; expecting his imminent death, he immediately bowed down and begged for pardon. King smiled and asked him, "Don't worry, you are safe. You have done nothing wrong. I know it is not only your question but everyone present here must be anxious to know about what has transpired to change my behavior. I will tell the secret of my transformation. Relax and take your seat." The king continued and told the story of change of his heart.

"As all of you know one of my dear friends is the king of a nearby small state. He is fond of hunting dogs. Whenever he wants to punish someone, he arranges a big show of execution. This serves dual benefit for him, one the victim gets executed, and the second he enjoys the brutal killing of an unfortunate person. I learned this trick from my friend and framed the rules to use dogs for punishing people who commit mistakes. The secret of my transformation is inspired by one of the incidents that he narrated to me.

My friend who is a king has a squad of dogs. As per rule any person who commits a mistake will be thrown to the dogs. The dogs shall be kept hungry for three days so they become ready to eat any person at any time.

Once he applied this rule on one of his ministers who gave him a wrong opinion. The rule was applied to all including his ministers. One Day, one of his ministers gave an opinion which later proved wrong. King ordered the soldiers to throw him to the hungry dogs. This was his final order. The minister pleaded begging the king, "Please I have served you for 20 years, pardon me once. I promise not to commit such a mistake in future."

King was adamant; he was not willing to lose the opportunity of an execution feast. Minister begged his pardon again and requested to delay his execution for ten days only.

The King thought for a while. Taking into account his long unblemished service of 20 years, he accepted his request and postponed execution for ten days.

The minister went to meet the trainer of dogs and requested him, "Please allow me to stay with dogs. I want to feed them for ten days only."

Previously the dog trainer was helped by the minister on many occasions. The dog trainer felt weird on his request but keeping in view his helping attitude he took the risk and said, "What will you gain? You are going to die soon."

The minister answered, "I shall find out soon."

For those ten days, the minister took good care of the dogs. He fed and washed them and offered all the comfort to them. He played, tickled and cleared their skin. For feeding, he took care of each dog. He used to sleep with them. In a matter, he lived like a dog in the company of dogs and befriended them all.

After ten days, the king came with his guards to the minister and said to him, "Now is the show time. I am anxious to see how your body will be ripped apart piece by piece by my famished dogs."

With the orders of the king, the minister was thrown into the cage of hungry dogs. The king was present with all his family members. All ministers, senior officials and some prominent people of his kingdom were also present to watch the event like the previous practice of such executions. Everyone was keen to see the spectacular devouring of a living human being by hungry dogs. When they were watching, the king, his family and soldiers were shocked to witness something strange.

Dogs were hungry but they all were standing silent and motionless. Some dogs were sitting behind the minister without harming him. The trainer of dogs was puzzled to see inactive dogs. It had never happened before that hungry dogs did not attack their prey instantaneously. Surprised over the behavior of dogs, he provoked and instigated them for attacking the minister. In turn, the hungry dogs started barking at him. The King was also puzzled to see the hungry dogs refusing to eat fresh flesh of a living being.

In anger, he asked the minister, "What have you done to my loyal dogs?" Never before these hunting dogs showed any mercy on their prey.

The minister was calm with no fear of hunting dogs. He answered the king back, "I have served these dogs for ten days only and they have not forgotten my service, while I have served you for 20 years and you forgot all of what I have done for you."

Everybody present there took note of what the minister had said. The act of dogs compelled the king to feel guilty.

The king declared that, "I also learned a big lesson of life from those dogs, who were used by my friend to instigate panic, terror and cruelty among his own subjects. This is the only secret for my transformation."

The Minister was released and all the futile and stupid rules of cruelty and apathy were canceled.

Let us always treat others in a compassionate manner and never forget the acts of kindness that are done to us.

We have the choice to spread goodness in the world and set an example for others.

Henry David Thoreau said, "Goodness is the only investment that never fails."

KNOW YOUR WORTH

Stop Thinking, Start Doing

by

NK Sondhi & Vibha Malhotra

The secret behind the success of most of the people is not what they do, but how they do it!

This book discusses the life-changing concepts through storytelling. You would find yourself closely connected to these stories. They will encourage you to explore your own potential to inspire you, and to achieve your real worth. This book will also help you to understand the traits that keep you from achieving your dreams. The book lays down a process to help you emerge from the clutches of negativity and develop a positive approach towards life.

By investing time in yourself, acknowledging your potential, setting a worthy goal, avoiding common traps, surviving bad days and harvesting the power of thoughts, you can be successful.

Read this interesting book to Know Your Worth.

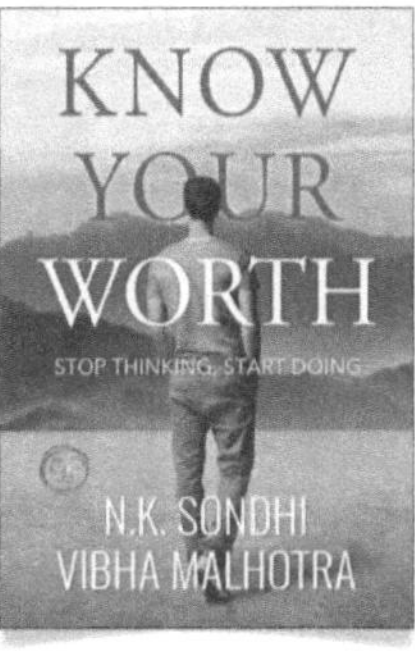

Price	:	Rs. 295
Pages	:	224
Size	:	8x5.25 inches
Binding	:	Paperback
Language	:	English
Subject	:	Self-Help
ISBN	:	9788180320231

Small Things Matter Most

Small Things & Habits Make a Difference

by

NK Sondhi

In life, we cannot always do great things—but we can do small things with great passion and love. This book discusses the ignored concepts about our small habits, small acts, and small events that happen every day in our life. Because of small problems we get lost in confusion and forget about our real goal of life. For want of big, we usually ignore and underestimate small things that play a vital role for big achievements.

The book will help to understand the traits that keep us away from achieving the pleasure of life full of human values. The importance of little things is embedded in our life. The need is to explore and implement them. This book will help readers to explore their individuality and attitude for a better and happy life. Robert brault said: "enjoy the little things, for one day you may, look back and realize they were the big things.

Price	:	Rs. 295
Pages	:	224
Size	:	8x5.25 inches
Binding	:	Paperback
Language	:	English
Subject	:	Self-Help
ISBN	:	9789389440966

OTHER BOOKS YOU MAY LIKE

- A Christmas Carol by Charles Dickens, ISBN: 9788193545874
- Anthem by Ayn Rand, ISBN: 9789389157079
- Apni Chhamta Pehchaniye by NK Sondhi, ISBN: 9788193545843
- As a Man Thinketh by James Allen, ISBN: 9788180320262
- Awakened Imagination by Neville Goddard, ISBN: 9789389157086
- Be What You Wish by Neville Goddard, ISBN: 9789387669550
- Becoming a Writer by Dorothea Brande, ISBN: 9789389157093
- Believe in Yourself by Joseph Murphy, ISBN: 9789388118385
- Civilization and Its Discontents by Sigmund Freud, ISBN: 9789387669499
- Feeling is the Secret by Neville Goddard, ISBN: 9789389157109
- Gita According to Gandhi by Mahatma Gandhi, ISBN: 9788180320040
- Gravity by George Gamow, ISBN: 9789388118484
- Great Speeches of Abraham Lincoln by Abraham Lincoln, ISBN: 9789380914336
- How to Attract Money by Joseph Murphy, ISBN: 9789388118408
- How to be filled with the Holy Spirit by A. W. Tozer, ISBN: 9789389157116
- How to Dev Self Conf and Imp Pub Speaking by Carnegie, ISBN: 9789387669000
- How to Enjoy Your Life and Your Job by Dale Carnegie, ISBN: 9789387669017
- How to Stop Worrying and Start Living by Dale Carnegie, ISBN: 9789380914817
- Julius Caesar by William Shakespeare, ISBN: 9789380914374
- Macbeth by William Shakespeare, ISBN: 9789380914343
- Madhubala by Manju Gupta, ISBN: 9789380914961
- Meditations by Marcus Aurelius, ISBN: 9789388118736
- Mein Kampf (My Struggle) by Adolf Hitler, ISBN: 9789380914855
- Metamorphosis by Franz Kafka, ISBN: 9788180320057
- Mother by Maxim Gorky, ISBN: 9788180320330
- My Experiments with Truth by Mahatma Gandhi, ISBN: 9789387669291

Develop your reading habit | **Gift books to your friends**

OTHER BOOKS YOU MAY LIKE

- My Inventions: The Autobiography of Tesla by Nikola Tesla, ISBN: 9789388118132
- My Life : Albert Einstein by GP Editors, ISBN: 9789388118941
- My Life : Dilip Kumar by GP Editors, ISBN: 9789388118934
- Quiz For All by Dr. Ruth Premi, ISBN: 9788180320897
- Romeo and Juliet by William Shakespeare, ISBN: 9789380914329
- Save Your Child by NK Sondhi, ISBN: 9789388118361
- Selected Short Stories of James Joyce by James Joyce, ISBN: 9788180320392
- Selected Stories of Rabindranath Tagore by Rab Tagore, ISBN: 9789380914770
- Sense and Sensibility by Jane Austen, ISBN: 9789380914589
- Tales from Shakespeare by Charles Lamb, Mary Lamb, ISBN: 9789380914367
- The Alchemy of Happiness by Al-Ghazzali, ISBN: 9789387669505
- The Art of Public Speaking by Dale Carnegie, ISBN: 9788180320422
- The Art of War by Sun Tzu, ISBN: 9789380914893
- The Autobiography of a Yogi by Paramahansa Yogananda, ISBN: 9789380914602
- The Autobiography of Benjamin Franklin by Ben Franklin, ISBN: 9788190276689
- The Bhagavad Gita by Sir Edwin Arnold, ISBN: 9789380914275
- The Canterville Ghost by Oscar Wilde, ISBN: 9789380914527
- The Dynamic Laws of Prosperity by Catherine Ponder, ISBN: 9789388118156
- The Game of Life and How to Play It by Florence S. Shinn, ISBN: 9789387669390
- The Great Gatsby by F. Scott Fitzgerald, ISBN: 9789380914473
- The Greatest Short Stories of Leo Tolstoy by Leo Tolstoy, ISBN: 9788180320002
- The Imitation of Christ by Thomas À Kempis, ISBN: 9789388118057
- The Invisible Man by H.G. Wells, ISBN: 9788193545850
- The Jungle Book by Rudyard Kipling, ISBN: 9788193545867
- The Knowledge of the Holy by A. W. Tozer, ISBN: 9789389157130
- The Law of Success by Napoleon Hill, ISBN: 9788180320927

Develop your reading habit | **Gift books to your friends**

OTHER BOOKS YOU MAY LIKE

- The Little Prince by Antoine De Saint-Exupéry, ISBN: 9788180320590
- The Magic of Believing by Claudie Bristol, ISBN: 9789388118149
- The Magic of Faith by Joseph Murphy, ISBN: 9789388118743
- The Miracles of Your Mind by Joseph Murphy, ISBN: 9788180320743
- The Origin of Species by Charles Darwin, ISBN: 9788180320453
- The Path of Prosperity by James Allen, ISBN: 9789387669512
- The Power of Awareness by Neville Goddard, ISBN: 9789387669406
- The Power of Concentration by Theron Q. Dumont, ISBN: 9789388118064
- The Prince by Niccolò Machiavelli, ISBN: 9789387669024
- The Prophet by Kahlil Gibran, ISBN: 9789380914022
- The Psychopathology of Everyday Life by Sigmund Freud, ISBN: 9789388118071
- The Pursuit of God by A. W. Tozer, ISBN: 9789389157147
- The Quick and Easy Way to Effe. Speaking by D. Carnegie, ISBN: 9789387669031
- The Seven Laws of Teaching by John Milton Gregory, ISBN: 9789387669413
- The Story of My Life by Helen Keller, ISBN: 9789380914541
- The Upanishads by Swami Paramananda, ISBN: 9789388118750
- The Wit and Wisdom of Gandhi by Mahatma Gandhi, ISBN: 9789380914039
- Think and Grow Rich by Napoleon Hill, ISBN: 9788180320255
- Thought Vibration by William Walker Atkinson, ISBN: 9789389157154
- Three Men in a Boat by Jerome K. Jerome, ISBN: 9789380914442
- Treasure Island by Robert Louis Stevenson, ISBN: 9788193545881
- Up From Slavery by Booker T. Washington, ISBN: 9789380914565
- Wake Up and Live! by Dorothea Brande, ISBN: 9789387669574
- Walden and Civil Disobedience by Henry David Thoreau, ISBN: 9788180320507
- Wuthering Heights by Emily Brontë, ISBN: 9788193545898
- Your Faith is Your Fortune by Neville Goddard, ISBN: 9789389157161

Develop your reading habit | **Gift books to your friends**

www.ingramcontent.com/pod-product-compliance
Lightning Source LLC
LaVergne TN
LVHW050416160726
843469LV00041B/1107

9789389716412